Christmas in Mouseland

Based on the stories by Katharine Holabird

Based on the illustrations by Helen Craig

Grosset & Dunlap

Angelina Ballerina™ © 2007 Helen Craig Ltd. (illustrations) and Katharine Holabird (text). The Angelina Ballerina name and character and the dancing Angelina logo are trademarks of HIT Entertainment Ltd., Katharine Holabird and Helen Craig. Reg. U.S. Pat. & Tm. Off. Used under license by Penguin Young Readers Group. All rights reserved. First published in the United States 2003 by Pleasant Company Publications. This edition published in 2007 by Grosset & Dunlap, a division of Penguin Young Readers Group, 345 Hudson Street, New York, New York 10014. GROSSET & DUNLAP is a trademark of Penguin Group (USA) Inc. Manufactured in China.

Library of Congress Control Number: 2006103286

ISBN 978-0-448-44663-9   10 9 8 7 6 5 4 3 2 1

Angelina held up a beautiful ball gown as she danced before the mirror.

"Careful, dear!" said Mrs. Mouseling, who was busy sewing ballet costumes. Miss Lilly's ballet class was putting on a special Christmas performance of *Cinderella Mouse* for Queen Seraphina of Mouseland.

As Angelina twirled, the gown swirled gracefully around her. "I can't wait to play the part of Cinderella Mouse!" she said excitedly.

"Don't forget that you have to audition for it first," Mr. Mouseling reminded Angelina as he stood the Christmas tree upright in the corner of the room.

But Angelina was so busy dreaming about the ballet that she scarcely heard her father.

On the way to ballet class, Angelina and her best
friend, Alice, spotted a poster for the *Cinderella
Mouse* ballet.

"Alice, do you think I'll get the part?" Angelina
asked hopefully.

"Santa Claus would choose you!" said Angelina's little cousin Henry, who was very excited about Christmas. He carried his stocking as he skipped along the snowy sidewalk.

When the mouselings reached the toy shop window, they pressed their noses against the glass and peered inside.

"Alice, look at the toy theater!" gasped Angelina. "It's wonderful!" Angelina could almost imagine herself dancing on the tiny stage. She gazed through the window long after Alice and Henry had run ahead.

At ballet class, Miss Lilly showed Henry how to dance the part of the little beetle that turns into a coachmouse.

"Now crouch down, Henry, then leap up tall!" said Miss Lilly, spreading her arms into the air.

But Henry couldn't concentrate. "Miss Lilly, does Santa Claus ring the doorbell?" he asked. "What if Santa Claus gets stuck in my chimney?"

Mr. Operatski, the famous director who was helping Miss Lilly with the ballet, leaped out of his chair. "This beetle will need a lot of work, Miss Lilly!" he grumbled.

"Henry will do fine," Miss Lilly said kindly. "And wait till you see his cousin, Angelina!"

Now it was Angelina's turn to dance. She leaped and twirled across the floor and finished in a beautiful pose.

"Charming!" said Mr. Operatski. "You certainly are the best mouseling to dance the part of Cinderella Mouse."

"But now," Mr. Operatski continued, "let's see who is the best mouseling to SING the part! The queen loves music."

Angelina's heart fell in her chest. She didn't like singing in front of everyone. She felt much too nervous.

Angelina took a deep breath and opened her mouth. "La-la-la-la . . ." she began. Suddenly, Angelina's voice squeaked. Priscilla Pinkpaws quickly covered her ears.

"Humph!" said Mr. Operatski. "Not quite the angel I had in mind. Angelina, you will play the Wicked Stepmouse!"

Angelina was *so* disappointed—especially when Priscilla Pinkpaws got the part of Cinderella Mouse instead.

Miss Lilly came to visit Angelina that afternoon. "There are many ways of being a star," Miss Lilly said gently. She set the Wicked Stepmouse's crown on Angelina's head. "You will be a marvelous Wicked Stepmouse."

Angelina practiced making wicked faces in the mirror, but she couldn't stop dreaming about playing Cinderella Mouse. Then she had an idea . . .

At rehearsal the next day, Angelina practiced the part of the Wicked Stepmouse. But instead of singing wickedly, Angelina sang in her sweetest voice. And instead of dancing big, bold steps, she danced gracefully.

Then, when Priscilla began her Cinderella dance, Angelina fell in beside her, performing the steps perfectly. Angelina danced her heart out.

"Stop!" said Mr. Operatski. "Angelina, did I ask to see you dance?"

"I'm sorry," said Angelina in a small, sweet voice. "I just couldn't help myself. This is my favorite dance!"

Mr. Operatski threw his arms into the air. "If Angelina is your best dancer," he said to Miss Lilly, "why can't she dance the part of the Wicked Stepmouse?"

Miss Lilly scolded Angelina. "Priscilla is playing the role of Cinderella," said Miss Lilly. "You will have to be happy with playing the Wicked Stepmouse."

"But it should never have turned out like this!" said Angelina.

"I'm sorry, Angelina," Miss Lilly said firmly. "But nothing is going to change, and the show must go on."

"Then it will have to go on without ME!" said Angelina. She burst into tears and rushed offstage, where she buried her face in her hands and cried miserably.

The next morning, Angelina heard laughter from outside her bedroom window. She saw Priscilla and her sister, Penelope, walking past the front gate. "Thank goodness Miss Lilly's going to play the Wicked Stepmouse," Priscilla was saying. "Angelina was hopeless!"

Angelina sighed and sank down beside the window, feeling very sorry for herself.

Mrs. Mouseling knocked gently on Angelina's bedroom door and asked, "Are you coming to breakfast, dear?"

"No," said Angelina sadly. "I'm not in any hurry now that I don't need to go to rehearsal."

But a little while later, Angelina came downstairs and slipped into her winter coat. "I'm going for a walk," she told her mother.

On the street outside, Angelina ran into her friend Sammy.
He was pulling a toboggan behind him. "Want to race the
Pinkpaws twins down Cheddar Hill?" Sammy asked Angelina.

Soon the toboggans were perched high atop the hill.
As they slid forward, Angelina crouched low. Angelina and
Sammy's toboggan gained speed, and they took the lead.

Just then, Angelina saw two figures walking along the sidewalk below. It was Miss Lilly and Mr. Operatski! Angelina tried to turn the toboggan, but it was too late. The mouselings crashed right into Miss Lilly.

"Oh, dear!" cried Miss Lilly as she struggled to stand up. "I'm afraid I've hurt my ankle."

Angelina knelt beside her teacher. "I'm so sorry, Miss Lilly," she said. Angelina felt terrible!

Now that Miss Lilly couldn't dance, Mr. Operatski wanted to cancel the Christmas ballet. Angelina found him at the theater, packing up his things.

"Please don't leave!" Angelina pleaded. "The show MUST go on—I'll dance the part of the Wicked Stepmouse. I can do it. I promise!"

Angelina convinced Mr. Operatski to stay. She called all the mouselings back to rehearsal. She even helped Henry learn to dance like a beetle.

But secretly, Angelina was worried. She hadn't had much time to practice her own part. Could she really do it?

On Christmas Eve, the Theater Royale was packed full. Angelina peeked nervously at the audience. She saw Mr. Operatski sitting beside Queen Seraphina, and just beside the queen was . . . Miss Lilly!

Angelina's heart leaped, and she danced into the spotlight. She flung her arms above her head and began singing in a loud, wicked voice.

At first, the audience booed the Wicked Stepmouse, but by the end of Angelina's performance, the audience cheered and applauded. "Bravo!" called Mr. Operatski as Angelina danced offstage and the red curtain came down.

On Christmas morning, Angelina stood before a very large present. "Go on," urged Mr. Mouseling. "Open it!"

Angelina ripped off the wrapping paper, and there was a toy theater like the one she had seen in the toy shop window. But this one was better, because Mr. Mouseling had made it look exactly like the Theater Royale!

"It's beautiful!" cried Angelina as she hugged her father.

And now it was Angelina's turn to give a gift.

Angelina held out the Wicked Stepmouse's crown for Miss Lilly, who was celebrating with the Mouselings. "Thank you for making this the best Christmas ever!" said Angelina.

"For me?" Miss Lilly asked warmly. "Thank you! Merry Christmas, my darling Angelina!"